The Traveler

BlΩΩds Divide Universe

a paranormal sci-fi series

by

Stacy McCarty

The Traveler

Bloods Divide Universe, Volume 1

Stacy McCarty

Published by Stacy McCarty, 2024.

No. 1 edition

WARNING: this book contents material which is not suitable for all audiences; mild sex, fantasy violence and other subject matter might trigger some readers please be advised.

This is a work of fiction. Similarities to real people, places, or events are entirely coincidental.

THE TRAVELER

First edition. December 11, 2024.

ISBN: 979-8227168986

Written by Stacy McCarty.

Also by Stacy McCarty

Bloods Divide Universe

The Traveler

Rapture of Men

Thorn

Pestilence

"When first my eyes came to rest upon your essence delight rolled, twisted, and danced inside my body.

Abruptly, my stomach sinks into the void of self-doubt.

Why must this crushing painful feeling resonate, like a criminal come to steal my dreams, my hopes, newly discovered?

All at once, both joy and shame collided, mix, and melt together leaving no evidence of hope revealed.

So I being weak, like the undeveloped neck muscle of a newborn, I crawl back inside myself unsatisfied and forever changed."

Prologue

I AM CAREFUL TO NOT be seen by the drones in the main hallway the last thing I need is to have a dagger after me for not following my guide's orders. But I'm not afraid I'm almost seventeen spins now and I'm sick on staying in my room all the time. It is not like anything will ever happen to me her in this huge fortress.

I kneel, out of breath fleeing from Dahlia. She is much quicker than me but I am smaller and I know where the secret passageways are.

"Aria!" Dahlia yells from off in the distant, darkened corridors.

I cover my mouth hoping to conceal the heavy, raspy sound of it. I realize that the sounds aren't coming from me but from one of the rooms. From the passageway, I can see into the other rooms. This is my only window out. Other then the occasional escape I make from Dahlia I am a prisoner. I have never freely walked outside of the fortress walls of the Kysco Nation. My eyes have witnessed the rise and fall of the three hues from inside these walls. Remaining on my knees I move closer to the door. I look through the small keyhole above the doorknob. The full view of the room comes into focus and I see movement inside. I grow excited, moving my face even closer for a better view. I am careful not to touch the door; I don't want to reveal myself to the occupants inside.

My excitement increases once I notice that one of the three bodies inside is a breeder. I am going to be a breeder one day soon too. I see that the breeder is male. His long torso is ripping and strong looking. I see the piece on a male that I have only heard about but never seen before him. He is covered in different markings which line his body. He stands and I see his beautiful skin which is bare, and covered by all the breeder's markers. The other two I now see are females as they both come into view. One of the women moves behind the breeder before she removes her robe. She is beautiful. Her hair is like gold and it's wavy like the ribbons on the drapes that hang in the grand hallways.

The breeder takes her hand placing it upon him and I watch him grow in size in her hand. I feel myself get a feeling in between my thighs that I haven't ever felt before now and in my belly unlike anything I've yet to feel.

I am forced to put an end to this urge by placing my hand over my heated lips. With one hand covering my mouth and my other hand pressed against my slit I eagerly stare at them as they touch, and I touch myself deeper. As they suck, lick, and bite I slide my hand down inside my undergarments. I only grow wetter and my feelings increase to the point that I whimper aloud.

I stop myself by pulling my hand out ending my pleasure for fear that they have heard me. I look through the keyhole, and see that they have not heard a thing, as they have all joined into a pile, twisting and turning around one another as they mate. Their moans are blissful encouragement to me.

"Aria!" Dahlia shouts while yanking me up, and off of the ground, bringing me eye to eye with her. My small feet dangling as she holds me like I'm merely feathers in her hands. "What are you doing here?" She demands in a quieter voice, but her eyes burn with rage for me. "Answer me, Aria!" She continues not waiting for a full moment to pass.

"I don't know what I'm doing. I am sorry." I pull out the first of many excuses. She places me on my feet on the ground in front of her as her eyes soften. "I am truly sorry...I won't..." I start but stop when we hear the doorknob behind me start turning.

"Come!" Dahlia snaps, grabbing me by the hand before rushing off down the corridor.

She moves fast, like the wings of the birds in the sky. I can't see her legs as she flies with me in hand. I can move fast too, just like she taught me, but I'm not like her nor is she like me. She is my Dahlia, my teacher and guide. I am the breeder, the source of life.

Ω

I attentively listen to Dahlia tell me the forbidden story of our old world as I try my best to fall asleep.

"In the darkest of the ether lays a world unlike any other, with both the power to destroy all; or create many wonders.

In a far-off land not unlike ours, tribes are divided, and families are separated; it is written that one female and one male from two different species, will right the wrongs, and undo the savage destruction of the Kysco Nation."

Chapter 1

The blue hue sat high in the sky cloaking the Kysco fortress in darkness. The golden towers stood lit up by the torches of the Kysco Nation and the lonely breeder sat with a plan in my head and a mean guide waiting to rid herself of me for the night.

Dahlia pulls the comb through my hair slowly gliding it down the back reaching the ends with a tug. I move trying to free myself from her grip. She growls a little at me but says nothing as she yanks me back into place. If only she wasn't so much stronger than I am. I move again this time not stopping until I'm standing. She moves to grab my hand but I'm quick and make it to my bed before she can stop me.

"Fine...sleep...it is time for you to rest now anyhow, Aria" she concedes with a smile. I think that she has even grown tired of this game. "Do you need anything before I go?"

"No." I answer. The only thing I can think of is escape; that's what I need. She smiles and moves to leave. "Wait...tell me that story again," I plea, remembering that I can't let her leave without this one thing that gives me hope.

"The story? What story?" She sits with a sweet smile almost taunt me. I want her to see me as the little girl that I once was; she's nicer to me when I'm that way with her.

"You know what story. Tell me about the Yukon Sea and the dark creatures and the magical flying creatures...flying what did you call them?" I pause forgetting what she had told me.

"Oh, that story. They're called Darjin and they can fly because they have wings." She explains.

"I want to see them for myself one day. I wish these were not just stories, Dahlia. How do you fly? You have no wings." I ask.

"I can't fly silly. I run. It only seems like I'm flying because of how fast I'm going. It's so fast it's like two blinks of your eyes." She adds before demonstrating by blinking her eyes twice. I laugh at her amused by her willingness to play. Tonight she seems so willing to play with me unlike most nights where she is very stern and without words for me.

"Will I get faster? Will I get stronger like you?" I press. She laughs while pulling my sheets up and over me covering my legs like I'm a child but I'm far from being a child.

"Yes, Aria you will get stronger, faster, and you will be a breeder which is the most precious of positions in our mighty nation. You should be very honored and proud to have such a great chance to give our world its next generation. The strongest generation, I believe." She says adding a wink at the end.

Ω

The sounds of crashing glass startle me awake. I move to get out of bed. I barely manage to wrap my robe around my body before racing over to the door to see and listen to the commotion in the hallway.

There is no keyhole so I must open the door slightly if I want to see who is in the hallway. I quickly open the door just enough to see out but no one can see it and I brace myself in front of the door just in case someone comes to the door and tries to enter.

Dahlia is the first person I see and next I see a huge man who is dressed in royal silk robes indicating that he is a royal council member. I notice the Kysco Nation symbol in crested in an amulet around his neck. I see broken glass on the ground surrounding their feet and it becomes obvious to me that he is punishing Dahlia for some reason.

"I don't care what you say, Dahlia you will get the girl immediately or you will face the heated end of my belt now go get her!" He shouts into her face spraying her with spit. And without even know this man I already hate him and never want to be with him.

"I can't get her, your royal highness she is not of mating age please forgive me but if you mate with a breeder too younger you two will surely breed a purged and no one wants to see that happen." She pleads him with her hands on his shoulders. He towers over her without speaking with fire in his eyes.

"Well, when will she be of age Dahlia? I know that girl is grown she's over nineteen years old stop staling me, Dahlia I will have my rightful mate and the power that comes with her too!" He snaps at her before pushing hands off of him. He moves towards my door but Dahlia moves in front of him blocking him.

"I understand that where you are from you track age differently but here under the three hues of Tragon we must adhere to the laws or our species will come undone." She urges while shaking her head.

"Move out of my way you stupid cow! Don't you know who I am! I am ultimate power and with my rightful mate ARIA I will rule this whole nation!" He shouts before trying to pass by Dahlia. She grabs his arm and pushes him back sending him sailing back ten feet. He lands and looks stunned as though he is surprised by her strength which he can't match.

"I'm sorry your highness but you must obey the laws and you must leave the breeder chambers immediately" She commands him.

I become too afraid to remain at the door so I race back over to the bed and get back in.

Dahlia enters my room frightened and out of breath. I have never seen Dahlia like this. She nods repeatedly as I move towards her. The most terrifying eerie feeling rolls through my body taking with it all my commonsense.

"You need to run, Aria. You will not understand what is going on and I don't have the time to tell you but if you stay there will be a war. Do you remember what I taught you about the Yukon and the Oldlands?" She asks and I nod. "It was all true; every, single, word I told you as a story was always your training, Aria. They wanted to take you years ago but I stopped them before. You are forty spins now and I can no longer hold them back from you." Dahlia demands keeping her voice quiet but her words ring loudly in my ears. "Run to the Yukon, you know the way I know you do." She stress almost out of breath.

"What—why aren't you coming with," I ask but I'm met with fierce hands which shove me towards my bedroom window. I struggle but she manages to get me over to the window all the same.

"I said run. Go through this window and follow the edge of the building until you come to the balcony. Once you are there I want you to stay out of sight, get yourself down the stairs, out into the main floor and leave this place. Whatever you do don't take the private corridors, Aria." She finishes with a fear in her eyes that scares me enough to let her hand go. I want to say no. I want to refuse her demand but her order also means I will get to finally escape.

"Yes, Dahlia I will do as you say," I agree. Wasting no time, I get myself out the window and gracefully scale the edge of the mighty fortress walls.

I watch Dahlia push her head back into the window and I lose sight of her. I turn my head facing the direction I need to go.

I try not to look down but my curiosity gets the better of me and I look immediately regret giving in. Below me is a drop that would surely end my short life if I miss one step and fall. I move slowly, placing every step with the upmost caution. All the time I'm wondering what would make Dahlia so afraid. What would cause her to put me in such a situation as this one?

I hear several varying sounds coming from all different directions inside. I move quickly and avoid looking down again. My bare feet

cling to the sliver of an edge as I round the last bit before I reach the balcony.

Chapter 2

"I can't believe that I'm back here either, Judy but you know how much my aunt meant to me and there's no way around it for some reason she insisted that I open her will at Troy Manor, something about being where the heart of the family was is what she told the family attorney." I answer while gesturing my fingers in quotations.

"If you need money Cadence then maybe you should get a job or something but don't go looking for some fortune from your past, trust me I remember just unhappy and down you become when you're around your family, Cadence. I don't want you to slip up, you know." Judy says through my cell phone and her words go unheard as I open the old door to Troy Manor.

"I am not after anything, especially money, Judy! What the hell are you talking about? Well would you think that about me?!" I spit onto my cell phone as the frustration of what she's saying rolls through me.

"Calm down...Cade, I didn't mean to upset you, you know I love you to pieces. I only want to see you happy. You're my best friend and I don't want to see you hurting again." She explains in a pained tone and I realize I've been too gruff with her.

"I'm sorry Judy, you and I go back at least ten years and I know that you only have my best interest at heart and I thank you for that." I try to apologize to my dear friend. Judy has been with me since I was sixteen or so and I don't know where I would have ended up without her as a friend.

"No I should apologize to you, Cade. You stopped my father from...you stop him from doing," her voice goes soft and fate as I can feel her struggling with the pains of the past, "well you know what you did for me, Cade." She adds as her voice returns to happier tone. "If you wouldn't have helped me by convincing your father into taking me in, I would have grown up on the streets or something worse."

"And I would do all over again, Judy you're like my sister. I love you to pieces. I wish you could have been here with me now. I don't know if I can handle this legal crap on my own, you're the brainy-yeck." I joke.

"You know I would have been there if I could have been but with Travis work schedule and my new work schedule I just couldn't get any time off. I'm sorry you have to bare this one alone, Cade. Are you there now?"

"Yes I just walked in and this place looks like it's been sitting empty for over old years or so. Nuts, right? I'll send you a picture so you can see what I'm talking about but I better let you go for now, Juds." I say as disconnect before her say bye.

Ω

I reach for the folded-up papers from my attorney but I miss and fall face first, smacking my face into my cherry wood desk.

"Damn...shit that hurt!" I scream while clutching my head in my hand. I can tell without seeing my forehead that there will be a bruise, maybe even a bump. I rub it while standing to get the papers I had wanted to begin with. "I really hope she didn't leave me with any bills, because there's no way I can afford to pay for shit. Maybe she did actually have money, I wonder if she left me some. How much money would she have? None, I'm guessing; she had nothing to give," I say aloud sending a muffled echo down the hallways.

I'm in my study. Or what remains of my study. Troy Manner has sat empty and unattended to for seven years now.

I open the letter. "Mr. Cadence Troy," I read, and then I say aloud, "Yeah. That's me. Yeah. Yeah. Wait! What?" I start pacing as the unreal news sinks into my already drunk brain. I continue reading, "...your Aunt Margaret was a very wealthy woman."

I pace over to the mini bar, reaching for something to drink before remembering that there's nothing there but dust. "I can't believe this. I did not know this."

I walk over towards my Grandfather Clock. The glare from the sun hits my face, blinding me briefly. "Shit...that's bright," I gasp. I look up at the clock noticing that it is still working underneath the layers of dust and dirt.

I push the dirt and dust off the face of the clock. "Well look at that; it's still working." I look down at my watch checking the time. "Holy shit the time is actually correct." I return my eyes to the clock as it strikes noon and sounds begin to chime throughout the room.

As the ringing sound hits my ears I feel my body start to vibrate. Slow at first but it increases by the second.

"What the hell is going on is there an earthquake?" I bellow to no one while grabbing onto the clock as if it could actually help me in some way. The clock keeps tolling and my body continues to shake and I feel a burning sensation coming from my chest.

I remove my shirt noticing that my neck-chain is glowing and it seems to be hot to the touch. I snatch it up in my hand yanking at it to try and remove it. Suddenly I feel my body move forward.

"What...what was that?" I move backward but my feet slide forward underneath. I look up as the clock blurs white, disappearing in front of me as what can only be described as a black hole emerges in its place. My legs are ripped out from underneath me as I slide through the hole and into the black void.

I look everywhere but see nothing discernible or describable as my brain bends around the new images flashing before my eyes. My skin feels like it's being smacked by a thousand hands all at once and until finally after several painful minutes my body becomes numb.

My body feels weightless and my hair blows upwards indicating to me that I must be falling. I begin to struggle. I wave my arms reaching for anything but finding nothing but darkness as I lose sight of my hands once their extended. Fearing the unknown I pull my arms back up out of the murky, dark void that surrounds me.

My ears start feeling like I have gone too high in altitude and my belly is twisting inside urging me to spill the contents within but I hold back somehow.

Without warning my body hits feet first into a warm, gooey substance and I become engulfed in it as it swallows me whole.

Ω

Darkness turns to light. I am laying on a black hard surface that feels and looks like marble. I can hear sounds coming from somewhere off in the distance. "Hello...hello is anyone there?" I whisper. I sit up with all my senses restored and I quickly stand. "I don't think that this is my basement..." I say to myself with what was left of my hope that I wasn't crazy and that I might have fallen through one of the old decrepit floorboards of Troy's Manor. I am standing in a hallway, on a black marble floor, dark-colored walls made from unrealizable materials. "Where the hell am I, actual Hell?" I gasp. I see a large window a few feet away and I race over to it. Peering out, I gasp at what I see. There are three planets, or moons, I don't know which. I stare, transfixed by the beauty of it all. "This is definitely not hell...but this isn't Montana either. I don't think this is even Earth." I add. My mouth drops open. I hear the sounds getting closer. "If this isn't Earth then those are probably not humans either so I'd better hide," I realize, before leaping into action and spotting a corridor. I race towards it, fleeing from the sounds.

"Stop!" A female voice demands. I stop in my tracks looking to my side.

"Shit...I don't want any trouble," I say with my hands in the air. I back up as she nears me I nod my head. "Look I don't know how I got here. Wherever here is? But I will leave if you could just show me how to get out of here." I scramble for help. She says nothing as she puts her hands on my face. I let her touch me almost paralyzed by her somehow. "You look like just a normal girl. You look human to me." I clear my throat as she moves closer.

"How did you do that? How did you appear from nowhere?" She asks while continuing to paw my face with her super cold hands.

"I don't know what that was that just happened. I don't even know where I am," I try answering. Her hand feels cold but soft. She is small, five feet two inches, and she looks at least twenty years old. Her hair is longer and is braided down her back. I can't tell the color of it because everything in the hallway is reflecting back the colors of those moons, even her hair. "Can you help me get out of here, ma'am?" I say taking her hand in mine I now feel the full chill of her skin causing me to drop her hand immediately. "What the fu—" I snap but I'm stopped by the return of the sounds of people nearing us. I move away from her turning without looking I dart forward hitting into a brick wall I see darkness and then nothing.

Ω

"You look unreal to me...who are you? What are you? I need to go home. The clock swallowed me whole, I think I need a drink." I mumble.

I open my eyes as flashes of her face and the sky above roll over me. I try moving but I feel trapped and I can't feel my feet. I realize that she is carrying me and that we are no longer in that hallway but outside somehow. My head throbs and a crushing pain moves through it.

Chapter 3

The strange male moves shaking his head again while I set him down on the shore of the Yukon Sea. He has been talking about unknown to me things. I don't think he is right in his head. His body is injured and he is bleeding from the head. I don't know what to do for him I pull a piece from my grown tearing it free placing it on his forehead. I wipe the blood while fully resisting my desire to lick up the blood with my tongue.

"Why do you smell so good, male?" I say to him but he doesn't respond and instead he continues to sleep. Every time I touch him I undergo a new feeling that begins to move through me, almost overpowering me but I hold strong resisting again the urge to lick and suck up his blood. I drop the damp and bloody cloth at his feet backing up towards the Yukon waters.

I turn racing into it dive head first into the shallow red water. Actually, if what Dahlia told me is true then this isn't really water at all but blood; blood that I can drink. It's the blood of Kysco Nation. I open my mouth filling it with my food and satisfy all my needs in an instant. My body, gown, and all are covered as I climb out walking slowly towards the strange male.

My desire to eat the male is gone and I return to his side placing the cloth back to his head. I pull back shocked as I realize that other then the blood on the cloth, his has no wounds on it that I can see. I look closer but see nothing on his head at all. "Why aren't you bleeding anymore?" I strain, continuing to lean further towards him. He moves again opening his eyes.

"What...what are you doing to me?" He yells while pulling away from me. "What are you? Where are we?" He shouts with his eyes trapping me in a hard grip.

"I've done nothing to you. Don't move you will hurt yourself again silly male." I snap trying to order this unintelligent male into shape. His face shrinks up a little like he doesn't understand which is to be expected from lower life form. "What type of Fae are you, male?"

"Stop calling me 'male' my name is Cadence Troy and I'm not a 'Fae' or whatever you just said I'm a regular guy... with a pounding headache," he snaps back at me with no respect in his voice like he doesn't know who I am or what I am.

I pull my hand away before bringing it back striking him across his cheek bone. The echo sounds up and down the shore shocking both of us. "Get yourself under control now, male Cadence Troy. You are representing 'Regular Guy' Nation so behave as such you will address me as Aria, just Aria I have no title." I add.

"Did you just hit me?" He asks.

"Of course I did. You were acting hysterical," I say. I move closer to his face to study him further.

"What...what are you doing now you going to hit me again or lick me?" He asks but I'm overcome by the smell of him and the feel of his skin. His hair is dark it seems in color, darker than mine but it is very short and parted on one side with some sort of substance keeping it place. He no top garments on him allowing me to see his chest up close. I not noticed his body before as I carried him to freedom and I'm not sure why I care to look now but yet I continue studying him. "Why are you just staring at me, Aria? You are making me feel very strange. This is too awkward don't you think?" He mumbles something to me that I care not to listen to. I have resisted him for far too long I want to bite him. I want to taste him. I push myself up onto his lap receiving no resistance from him.

"Aria...your name is...Aria? Why do I feel like I can't move right now? I just want you to..." He groans as I caress his shoulders with my eyes fixed on his neck. The sound of his blood flow pulls me to him until my lips are on his bare flesh. "Why...wait..." He tries again to speak his eyes transfixed on me as I end my painful need by biting down into his neck. My teeth have never bitten before but my body naturally responds to it, and it's as if I've done this all along.

His body goes lump in my arms and he holds still as I pierce his skin with my extended teeth causing his blood to spill into my mouth. The sweetness of the favor overpowers me and I moan loudly while continuing to drink his blood. I feel his head slump to the side. I pull back lifting my teeth out of his skin causing them to reject back to normal size again.

"Oh no, please don't be dead. That shouldn't have hurt you nor should it have killed you." I say while gently moving his head with my hands. "But then again you are not from this world, I believe, and no not your anatomy." I began to worry just before he moves slightly and I see his eyes are open. "Good you are alive." I cough and fill of relief for some reason. My excitement returns but I don't plan to drink again. I want to do other things to him. I can feel that his body is strong but he isn't a match for me. The heat from his body is intoxicating I feel almost drunk from him. As I feel his blood course through my body I start to sense a deeper part of him, his emotions start to fill my body somehow and they are overwhelming.

"Aria, why does this feel so good to me, this should feel painful or something, right? I mean you just bite my neck. How does this feel so good," he says before pressing his lips to mine snatching my reality away from me.

I fall into his mouth willingly. His hands find my waist and he unfastens my gown before pushing his hands inside to touch me. Everything is happening so fast but I can't gain my strength to stop myself.

"Uh...ah...Cadence!" My raspy voice pleas but he does not listen, rather he places his hand on my most intimate spot and I realize that somehow my bite must have an intoxicating effect on him as he seems powerless to resist touching me.

"Grrr!!" I hear horrific growls off in the distance.

"Stop!" I stammer into his mouth before breaking free from him standing up. My mind starts racing as I recognize the growls of the Zerkers and I know we must go immediately. "Come on, get up we have to go now or we will become dinner," I add before offering my hand to help him up.

"I got it. I can still stand up on my own," he says, before trying to stand but he only manages to get up onto one knee.

"I believe you got it but you will need to practice later. Let me help you for now, Cadence." I offer again to which he takes my hand freely. I grab his hand yanking him up not wanting to waste time.

"GRAWL!! GRAWL!!" The growls are getting closer.

"What is making that sound? It sounds like really pissed off wolves or something," Cadence says before he shows me his teeth with his cheeks pressed outward, and in that second, I feel warm on the inside for the first time.

"Those are the sounds of the Zerkers and if I'm not wrong they are on their way to us right now so we must run from here are we will die for sure." I try to warn him again.

"Zerkers, what is a zerker? Wait, I don't think I want to stick around long enough to find out, Aria. But I'm afraid that your right I don't think I can run just yet. I don't understand why my legs won't move correctly right now. I think it has something to do with the atmosphere here. What is this place, Aria?"

"This is Tragon, and you are standing on the shores of the Yukon Sea alongside the Kysco Nation. You were just in the Kysco Fortress, home to the Royal Council, Cadence of Troy." I try to explain our land to him further.

Chapter 4

As I move with this stranger down this beach, I feel almost like I'm on a vacation. Like some normal traveler out on an excursion with a friend. Aria's small, slender body moves alongside mine before turning to me.

"We must hurry. You need to stop slowing down. I have not heard the zerkers for sometime but we should still keep moving it's not safe out in the open like this." She says before looking away. I remain quiet and try my best to keep pace with her. *Now I wish that I really was on a vacation so I could order up a drink and take a sit on this beach on this distance planet.*

We've walked for what seems like five miles at a very quick pace. *This girl can move unlike anyone I have ever seen.* My only aid was the soft cushiony feel of the sand underneath my shoes which was preventing blisters from forming on my feet. This wasn't something that I'm accustom to back home, all this running and feeing creatures that I can only hear.

I have been watching these three moons move from one side of the Yukon Sea to the middle part of it. This leads me to wonder if these moons ever actually set. I hope not because they are the only source of light here for what I can tell. The purple, yellow, and blue colors of the moons are having a calming effect on me somehow I have noticed. It reminds me of a lava lamp from the 70's or something like that.

The truth is that I'm craving my fix. My daily blood alcohol levels are bottoming out and I'm having real feelings. Feelings about my shit-filled life from before when I was beyond the veil back on earth.

I bring my foot down one more time before stopping in protest. “Wait a minute! I need to rest.” I demand before yanking my hand free from her cold hand’s grasps.

“We must not stop. There is no time for resting, uh...” She pauses as if she has forgotten my name already.

“Did you just forget my name, Aria? I’m not moving my feet out of this sand. If this even sand, I don’t know where I am nor do I have any idea where you are taking me.” I snap with a finger in her small, round face. She slaps my hand down. I try to resist her but her strength is intense and unlike a human beings’. I plant my feet in the dark brown sand in an attempt to send a message.

“This is the Yukon Sea and this is Tragon you are standing in the Kysco Nation land.” She snaps back while pointing around us before reaching for me again and I dodge her once more. “Fine, if you won’t move than I can carry you again if you would prefer?” She says with a half smile. She moves towards me and I lean backwards barely missing her grip.

“And?”

“What else do you need to know?”

“Where are we going? Where are you taking me, Aria? I don’t know you at all I’m not going to blindly following to my own death.”

“We must go to the Shylo Tribe ruins. That is all that I can tell you for now because that is all that I know. Now Cadence, will you please come along with me before the zerkers eat us alive?”

“I will walk on my own but only after I rest and drink.” I demand with my eyes flexed on hers. “Aria, I need to drink and eat something, anything please.” I add with a small nod she nods back. “You understand that I need to eat, right? If I don’t eat or drink water I can’t walk, my body won’t let me.” I say. She moves away heading towards the rocks lining the shoreline.

“I will find water for you, Cadence.” She says with her back to me. “I will look for food as well but I don’t think I will find much. Stay here close to the Yukon Sea waters you should be safe for now. I hope. *(She says under her breath)* I haven't heard the zerkers for quite some time like I said maybe they have found another food source instead of us." She adds.

I freeze in my tracks once she says food source. For a moment I had forgotten about the strange zerkers she was talking about earlier. I do as she instructs and head over to the bloody looking waters of the Yukon Sea careful not to touch it or let it touch my shoes. I look out over the rippling red waves thinking about my life. I can't help but be reminded of the sweet taste of red wine and delicious Merlot while watching the waves splashing the shore. I lick my lips thinking about cupping my hands together and scooping up some of the sea water. I reframe knowing it's not wine but I do wonder just what it is and why is the water red?

"It's not wine, stupid!" I say aloud. I lean down examining the water further. "Why is it red and it looks thick too?" I cup my hands together and pool the water into the palm of my hand. "It definitely isn't water it looks like blood." I smell it before pulling back dropping the liquid from my hands. "Yuck! It is blood! What is going on, why is there a bunch of blood pooled together like this?" I stand backing up. "She called this the Yukon Sea. I think she even dove into it earlier like she was happy to be in it, like she was drinking the blood or something." I turn around to look for her before looking back at the bloody sea. "She's some kind of blood-sucker isn't she? She bit me earlier. It felt amazing but still she bit me and that's a little stranger than I'm used to. Why did it feel so good? Her smell and her body seem to steer up my sexual desires something that the ladies back home haven't done it a while. Ha-ha!" I stop and laugh at myself.

Chapter 5

It is afternoon now and we should be safe from the night creatures. I turn back looking towards the Yukon Sea. My body is tired. My stomach is empty and my head is filled with images of Dahlia's face. I had never seen her look that scared. Come to think of it I've never seen Dahlia afraid ever. Forty spins have come and gone and not once has my attendant, my teacher and guide ever looked afraid. I turn my focus back to the ground and the Shylo berries which surround my feet. At least I hope that these are Shylo berries, I have no real point of reference seems how I don't ever require the consumption of anything other than the waters of the Yukon Sea. Never the less I believe that these white blossoms with wide stems are the berries she described.

"I will hurry and pick as many as I am able to carry." I say aloud while bending to scoop up the berries into my arms. I should probably get him something to drink in additional to the food. I look around. There are rows of berry covered hills for miles. I spot a small sproutshroom. I walk over to them peering down at them spotting the poled water in the shrooms centers.

"How will I get the water back to him without losing most of it?" I say aloud as I think for a moment longer before marching back down to the shores. I see Cadence with his back facing me. As I near him he seems to be staring out at the sea like he can see someone he knows swimming in the water.

"I have found you something to eat." I say, startling him as he turns shocked to see me. I feel slightly silly holding food for this male and so I shave the berries into his chest allowing him barely a chance to grab them from me before they can drop.

"Shylo berries are very filling." I say. He makes a strange face before biting into a hand full of the berries. I watch his expression as he chews. The slight changes in his face are fascinating to me. He seems to have so many different faces. "Do you like them Cadence of Troy?" I ask. He nearly spits out his mouth full before he starts laughing. I grow angry and remain confused.

"Yes...I do like the berries, thank you." He says. His round brown eyes widen as he stares at me.

"Stop laughing at me than." I say as he continues to giggle while finishing off the berries.

"Sorry Aria I'm not laughing at you. I'm laughing at what you just now called me." he explains in a lower tone that offers a soothing effect on me.

"There is water for you to drink too." I offer. His eyes widen. His head nods violently. "Please follow me I will show you where the water is." I add before moving away from him and I can feel he is on my heels following me. I feel his breath on the back of my neck. It's warm and quick. He is taller than me and something about that makes me excited. Like that maybe he is strong, fierce and that maybe he can handle himself in a battle. I had never thought about a man before now. My mate will be one of council members for what I've been told. I will not choose them rather I will be chosen. His scent is growing stronger, more musky and sweaty, I like it. I like his smell. And I sure liked the way he tasted. We arrive at the sprout summit and I point down at the pooled water. "See...water for you to drink." I soften my mouth turning the corners upwards matching one of his earlier expressions.

"So it is water and it's safe to drink than?" He asks while looking down before looking back at me matching my expression and I feel a wave of laughter push its way out of me.

"Well Aria I don't believe it this looks just like an upside down mushroom filled with water." He adds before leaning down cupping his hands together to scoop the water to drink. "Now if only you could find me some new clothes so I can get out of this shirt and dress slacks." He chuckles while looking down at his attire.

"You can disrobe if you would like. I do find it interesting that you are wearing so many garments to begin with. Are you attending a special ceremony later?" I ask without thinking. He stands with a sober look like his stomach is turning and he's going to be ill. His eyes are cold and his matched expression is erased. I must have said something to upset him.

"Actually I was attending my aunt's funeral earlier this morning." He pauses briefly. "This morning seems like a life time ago now." He adds before walking a few feet away while looking around the valley. "Where the hell is this place anyways? What have I gotten myself into here, Aria? This place seems to have three moons and no sun. One blue moon, one yellow moon, and one purple moon all of which shine the most amazing hues of color as far as the eye can see. I don't even know what time of day it is. I assume that I have been gone for at least a few hours or maybe more." He finishes and looks at me.

"I don't know which one of your many questions I should try to answer first Cadence." I say while remaining very confused by the names for the things around us.

"Please stop calling me that, only my parents and strangers call me by my full name. Call me Cade."

"Cade..." I repeat. I like how his name rolls off my tongue. He nods. "Well Cade, you are in the Shylo Valley alongside the Yukon Sea." I answer but I'm only half certain that I'm correct.

"This place looks a lot like back home, aside from the moons, of course."

"But we are not safe here out in the open. Soon it will be night and only the blue hue will shine." I warn as I point up at the hues which have already started to transcend into the beyond. I haven't heard the zerkers for some time now but that doesn't mean that they have gone away, they could still be on our trail. We will need to mask our scent in the Shylo Valley. The berries should cover up our scent." I add. I hold back the fact that I have never seen this valley with my own eyes. I am just like him at this point; a stranger in a strange land. I have only heard of these places. These places that were only fantasy in my head up until this morning, and then suddenly my whole world changed in a flash. Now I'm alone, or not really alone but this stranger is not my kin nor can he help me. He can't even keep pace with me and we will have to be fast if we stand a change at night out here on the tundra. I feel his hand on my shoulder. I bring my gaze back to his face. His eyes are wider then before and he is showing his teeth in the most peculiar way. His fingertips press down gripping me in place while he lowers his head bringing us face to face.

"What the hell is in these berries?" He rattles. His voice is pitchy and fast. I notice his brown eyes seem to be spinning in their sockets. I remain silent unsure how to answer him. I don't want him to know just little I know about this world I call home.

Chapter 6

I feel as though I have drunk twenty cups of coffee after snorting a line of coke. My body is energized times hundred. I feel my hands start to shake.

"Seriously, what's in these berries, Aria? Are they like coffee full of caffeine? They seem to be filled with caffeine or something like it because right now I think that I could run for forty miles without resting." I say. I remove my hand from her shoulder which I hadn't noticed I had placed on her. She steps closer. Her small frame holds my attention as I look her up and down. She is practically the size of a child and I'm over twenty years old hardly a good match. But she seems stronger than I am. And it is clear to me that she isn't human even though she appears to be. The coldness of her flesh is one indication and her speed. Her soft but frozen skin somehow draws me into her.

"I am glad to hear that the Shylo berries have nourished your body, Cade." She says. I get a jolt in my stomach when she says my nickname. It doesn't help that her grown barely covers her chest and the slits up the sides of her dress opens up revealing her legs and her hips. And I'm pretty sure that she isn't wearing any undergarments. I immediately push the wild thoughts out of my head.

"I'm ready to go now."

She turns looking into the vast distance. "We will need to get away from the Yukon Sea the water attacks too vicious creatures at night. I think we should head away from it and go through the Shylo Valley." She finishes. She turns and starts walking. I join her easily matching her pace. I can't help but steal another peek at her from my peripheral vision. I don't want her to feel uncomfortable with me by staring at her. I'm certain that she is used to all the attention and stares by how beautiful she is.

"So you're some kind of leader or princess than from the sound of things?" I ask her without looking at her.

"No, I am neither a leader nor a princess, I'm not sure what a princess is but I'm that. I am a breeder. I am one of the chosen." She explains with a great deal of confidence.

"What is a breeder? I mean what is entailed in that title?" I ask but by the name I have a feeling I already know what she might be in store for.

"I am to breed with the council member who chooses me..." She starts to add but I stop in my tracks not moving.

"What the hell are you saying? You're supposed to be chosen to breed with someone?" I emphases the word *breed. Does she mean mate, have sex with? What kind of sex slave fortress did I land in here?*

"Yes, I am the breeder so of course I will do my duty when it is time. But for now I must find the Shylo Temple and wait for Dahlia to come find me there." She adds before returning back to a quick pace leaving me behind in a leap. I quickly join her, shocked but determined to get further answers.

"Who is this Dahlia anyway?"

"She's my teacher and my guide. She has been with me for as long as I can remember."

"Back there..." I ask. She nods. "In that huge castle or fortress, you were born there and you were raised there too?" I press and she nods. "Who is the royal council?" I ask and she stops in her tracks.

"We must run Cade I can hear the zerkers coming." She urges while looking at me this time I see actual fear in her eyes. "I understand that it probably bothers you to be carried but I must get us to safety and you are simply too slow." She says as I dart off at my quickest sprit pace leaving her behind.

I almost chuckle but I stop as I feel my body lifting up off of the ground. In mid-air I notice she's by my side almost mocking my efforts while she's holding me up by my arm. I stop resisting her allowing her to hold on to me while continuing to run at a speed so fast that I feel more like we're flying than running. The adrenaline races through my body as I fight to maintain consciences. Something about the press of this planet's atmosphere and the speed at which she traveling must be affecting my equilibrium. She seems unfazed almost in her natural state, like a wild cheetah running on the vast tundra of Africa. She's of course much faster than a cheetah. The stimulating effect of the berries continues pumping through my blood, and it's like I'm drunk. The shrubs, rocks, and brushes become merely a blurry backdrop as we sail across like a schooner on the ocean. The only few pleasures I had as a teen was the summers I spent with my grandfather out at sea on the families' schooner. Even at a competitive speed of sixty-five knots Aria would have sailed pass us with ease.

Ω

We fully stop after hours of her doing the leg work. We arrive at a small clearing surrounded by ten foot rock formations. The ground is covered with soft grass like shrubs. I sit down to rest.

"Aria, come and sit down and rest you must be exhausted." I say as I pat the ground next to me. I look up at her and the rocks grab my attention. "I swear those rocks look like there were put here intentionally for some sort of ritual or ceremony. Where are we now, Aria, are we on the Shylo tribes' lands?"

"No, we are still too far west. We are still on the Kysco tundra and still very much in danger. I must check the perimeter to make sure it's safe first, you rest." She explains before vanishing.

"And she's gone like that!" I snap to myself. I lay back placing my arms behind my head. I stare up at the sky which looks like a tropical fruit punch drink stirring around my head. The bright colors are breathtaking. I let out a loud sigh. "What am I doing? I just blindly go off with a strange young woman, who carries me off into the wildness. I truly am insane." I pause as I notice a shooting star. "Shit! Wow the sheer spender of this place was worth the trip through that black hole or whatever it was. I'm not even experiencing any withdrawal from the booze it's kind of nuts. It's been at least twelve hours since my last drink. My anxiety is gone too. My constant stress seems to have subsided maybe the shock and excitement of the experience..." I stop to prompt myself up onto my elbows looking forward. I see a flash cross in front of me before I notice it's her as she sits next to me.

"I'll never get used to your speed. It's like magic. I thought you were moving fast while carrying me before but just now I'm pretty sure you traveled so fast that I couldn't see you. You were invisible to me." I say with my eyes on her.

"Magic...what is that?" She asks. Her face all bunched up letting her adorable innocence seep out. Suddenly it's as though all of her assumed power is merely an illusion that my alcoholic minds made up.

"I don't think that I'm smart enough to explain to you exactly what magic is but I'll try." I say while trying not to stumble over my words. She leans closer. "Magic is like making the invisible visible and impossible possible. I guess." I finish before chuckling at my half-ass attempt at being smart. I'm the dip-shit Stanford drop out. Not because I couldn't understand the material. I dropped out of school because I was too stupid to care about learning more. I was a fool back then, a rich, young, and from a powerful family so working hard wasn't my thing. I thought that I could skate by on all that in instead of earning it through constant action. In that regard she's smarter than me already at her age.

Chapter 7

I watch him carefully as he attempts to explain yet another new term of his to me. I do not understand why he talks to me as though I am a child when it is clear that I'm the one caring for him in this situation. But I listen to him giving him respect and attention just like Dahlia told me to show to those who are simple minded like Cade clearly is. I study his shape as he talks. He is steady and tall. His scent excites me but I don't understand why. I have not gotten the urge to bite him again but I want to be close to his body this urge is concerning to me. I should not want anything to do with him in that way. *Or is this feeling I'm having normal?* Cade is a man after all. Maybe his scent is only confusing to me because of that fact. Either way I should keep my distance less I forget myself should my urges return.

He removes his top garment baring his chest. I notice his markings on his arms and back. He has different symbols and shapes that are beautiful and striking.

"What tribe are you from?" I ask as I point to his body.

"Huh? What do you mean by that?" He says before removing the covering on his feet. I start to wonder if I too should remove my garments as he is doing. He looks down at his markings and then he back at me. "These are just silly meaningless pictures. Nothing more than that I assure you. I'm no member of any tribe." He adds. His expression changes as if there's pain coursing through him.

"You have no tribe? Everyone has a tribe, Cade. I'm sorry to hear that you do not have one of your own." I say.

He turns his attention on the sky and grows quiet. I try to look elsewhere but my eyes stay glued to him. His skin is darker colored then mine. It almost matches his brown eyes. His lips were soft, delicious and the memory of them on mine is resurfacing as he looks back at me again.

"I'm not the least bit tired, must be those berries that have me so wired and restless." He says. He stands and starts pacing, looking nowhere in particular. "So where are we? What is this place?" He asks again and I start to wander if his memory is bad. I feel as though I must remain quiet or I'll only be lying to him. "Hello...Aria?" He adds loudly making me jump a little.

"I don't know!" I let slip. I realize my error and I quickly stand pacing in the opposite direction as him. I don't see him stop and being to follow me.

"What do you mean you don't know, Aria?" His voice licks my ear and I turn coming face to face with him.

"I have only heard stories of these places. I don't know anything beyond the fortress walls. What Dahlia taught me was forbidden. But I think that I can get us to the Shylo Temple. And once we are there than we will wait for her to come and get me. I will help you get back to your home once Dahlia finds us." I lie. I hate lying. He nods before sitting back down. I move and join him.

"Does it seem to be getting darker or am I just imagining it?" He asks while looking to the sky.

"Yes, it is almost nighttime, Cade and the two hues will set leaving behind only the blue hue." I answer while pointing to the hues in the sky above. "Don't you remember, Cade I told you this earlier when we were by the Yukon Sea?" I ask but he shakes his head indicating that he doesn't. "See look," We watch as the yellow and purple Hues slip into the world's end disappearing into the distance. The valley grows dark. He starts shriving.

"Oh Jeeze, it's really cold now, like really cold. Did the temperature go down twenty degrees or what?" He grabs up his garments quickly putting them back on covering his bareness.

"Oh yes that's right you're a lot like the royal council in that way, your skin requires warmth I understand." I conclude. He raises his brow.

"Oh great you are comparing me to those gang raping royal council members that you seem to worship? No thanks." He shakes his head.

"I do not understand your silly terms for things." I mark while putting my arms around his body holding him in place. "I will offer you my warmth, Cade that way you will not freeze in the night." He begins to laugh at me and I grow angry. "Stop!"

"Stop what Aria laughing at the absurdity that you could possibly keep me warm. You're as cold as ice to the touch and your gorgeous body is tiny and not big enough to block the wind. But I love that you are attempting to take care of me." He says while wrapping his arms around my body. My body feels like it is melting under his touch. I lose my ability to stop myself from moving closer to him as our chest touch. I feel my nipples harden. His scent is overwhelming me now and him being so close I can no longer back off my urge to taste him again. But he beats me to it by placing his lips to mine. I meet him with increased pressure and I feel his tongue slipping inside of my mouth. It feels unlike anything else. My body seems to come to live, moving on its own following his lead. He lays me back onto my back and gets on top of me. His hands start moving slowly down my ribs on each side making me sigh. I feel myself getting wet between my thighs unlike when I touch myself. I don't want to stop. I can't help but let it happen. The pleasure I'm feeling is exquisite but I must keep us safe from the night creatures which will surely come now that it is nighttime. I'm almost afraid to speak because I don't want him to stop. I move my hand onto the flesh of his arms so I can feel it against mine. His body's heat gives me pleasure. He kisses down my mouth moving onto my chin and then to my neck. I sigh loud, unable to control myself. He must be a master at this. The warmth of his tongue on my neck gives me chills. I start to shiver underneath his warm body not because I'm cold but because it feels so good.

"We should..." He starts to say through kisses but then he stops as he continues gliding his tongue down my collarbone. I part my legs allowing his hips to decent deeper into my hips and now I feel his hardness. I can hear his blood pounding faster as it races to his groin and the last thing I want to stop.

Chapter 8

Her skin tastes like honey and sweat cream gliding across my tongue. I can't help myself. I feel her body shaking underneath mine as she response to my touches. She's primed and willing I know it but I'm not going to be the one to take it from her.

"Aria, I don't know what's come over me," I say while continuing to kiss her.

"It's not your fault that you are being drawn to me without a choice. My bite earlier makes it next to impossible to resist me." She says. "That's my best explanation. Truthfully, I have never experienced this before so I have no idea what is happening to me or you. (Dahlia had told me that all breeders can control there mates' desire for them)." She says. I pull back away from her.

"What do you mean by control my desires?" I stop her on that word because right now I feel under some kind of control beyond my own.

"But she never taught me how to do this so I can't be controlling you. I want to tell you so much more about the things that I have been taught but it is forbidden to tell an outsider anything about the personal life of a breeder. Nor can I tell you about the details about the royal council even know I have already slipped up and told you that you look and dress like them. Maybe that's why you are so attracted to me. I wish Dahlia was here so I could ask her about what is happening to the both of us." I say before he starts to kiss me again.

"I don't wish that at all because if she was here she'd probably have me executed or something for even touching your soft but cold skin." He says as he caresses my arms no longer kissing me. "I have a strange question for you, Aria. What do you normally eat? I only ask because I noticed that earlier you seemed to have been drinking the waters of the Yukon Sea. Which by the way the water looks and smells like blood? Is it blood?" I say.

"I don't think your questions are strange at all. I eat only the water from the Yukon Sea. All though I have never had to go to the actual sea to drink it, it was always just brought to me for consumption. This is the first time that I have ever drunk from someone before. I am sorry if I hurt you in anyway. I was so overwhelmed I had not thought about whether or not I was hurting you." She says.

"It didn't hurt, no. I just feel better than I have ever felt before. Like you shot me full of some super powerful drugs that make me faster and my head is clearer." I say. She smiles the brightest smile. "You have a very beautiful smile, Aria."

"Smile, is that what I'm doing with my face?" She says as she continues smiling.

"Yes you are smiling and it is beautiful." I say holding back from saying too much.

"I'm starting to feel funny about this now and the way you are looking at me makes me think that you've never seen anything beautiful before. Cadence, are you going to be mated to a female back where you are from?"

"No way! I'm never getting married or anything close to it, Aria. Hell, I feel bad for you because it sounds like you have no choice but to get married. Not me, I have a choice and I say no way." I say before starting to laugh.

"I don't understand why this question is funny to you? Nor do I understand why you never want to a mate. Why would anyone knowing not choice a mate?" She asks. I'm dumbfounded and pause briefly thinking how best to answer her without coming off as crazy or a jerk.

"Because back where I come from marriage and mating as you call it isn't the highest on my to do list. Not all men want to get married because we enjoy our freedom. Plus, don't get me started on having kids subject either. I'm really not trying to have any kids anytime soon, if ever."

"Children?" She asks.

"Yes children. I don't think I can handle them at all. I'm much of a kid myself. It wouldn't be fair to have some little person relying on me for anything. I'll only disappoint them I think." I look away from her no longer laughing now that I'm thinking about all my mistakes. "Stop with all these questions. I must stop kissing you too!" I say in protest pulling myself up off of her bringing my body into a standing position. I avoid looking at her as I quickly put my shirt back on. I fear if I look at her while I'm still so weak that I will throw myself back down on top of her and I won't stop until I've had her.

"Have I offended you, Cade?" She groans.

"No, not at all, Aria I'm afraid I'm the one who is out of line here." I turn to her noticing she's up now on her feet. "I should not have kissed you to begin with. I don't know why I did that. I shouldn't take advantage of your innocents." I add. I move towards her to offer her some comfort but she backs up suddenly with her eyes wider.

"Quiet! I hear something!" She commands with her eyes fixed on the darkness behind me like she can actually see into its vastness.

"What is it? Do you see what it is making noises?" I turn around just as she passes me. She stands in front of me with her arms raised up preparing for a fight. I hear echoed howls off in the distance. "I heard that! What are they?" I try not to sound scared but I'm terrified.

"Get back, stay behind me Cade no matter what happens stay where I can get to you." She says. I nod unable to speak. I see them. Several darken furry beings making their way towards us at an alarming speed. "Get back up against those rocks. There is at least five or more of them from what I can see." She adds.

Seconds pass and from the shadows emerges four large dog-sized animals in front of us. They are growling and snapping their teeth. Two of them lunge at Aria at once as she darts effortlessly to the side missing their attack. They spin wildly around dodging back at her again but she spins to face them grabbing one by the neck with her hands, as she snaps its neck with ease. I notice that she's different looking. Her eyes are no longer sweet and innocence but instead their blackened with all the whites gone. She grabs the two animals picking them up and tossing them off into the distance. One lands, rolling and stunned while the other one jumps up racing back at her. Before it reaches her it cries out in pain and drops dead at her feet. Another one drops as well behind it and the last one drops in its tracks as well. She moves towards it noticing arrows in its body. She yells out to me.

"They are all dead!" I race towards her but I'm stopped by a piercing pain in my back. I feel sharp claws on my back and shoulders as I feel my flesh split open. The pain is unbearable. I turn to see but I'm met with claws on my face. The teeth bite down into my skin and I hear my bones crack. I can hear muffled sounds around me. My heart pounds in my chest but my eyes go dark and I can't see anything.

"Help!" I stammer with blood in my mouth. I put my hand out and feel teeth on them, bending them and cracking them into what feels like thousands of prices. "Stop! Stop!" I gag. I feel the animal's teeth on my shoulder and I know that if I don't get lose now that this will be it for me. I take up what little strength that's left in me to turn onto my side and without explanation a power surges through me and I'm freed by my own unexplainable strength. I look down and watch as my hands turn into fierce claws which shred the next animals throat clear through in seconds. My voice changes and I roar out like a wild cat. My spine is arched and fur has replaced my skin. I see Aria but she looks taller than me as she stands by my side covered in the blood of those creatures. We are both soaked in blood. We prepare for another attack from the last of the fierce pack. Two figures appear from behind us, shooting arrows into the remaining animals killing before they can reach us. I can smell them and hear them better than ever before. I am aware that I'm no longer a human as the darkness circles in my head while I grow dizzy.

"Cade, are you hurt? What's happening?" Aria gasps. The darkness takes me in and I loss conciseness.

Chapters 9

I stand in a field of bloody bodies confused and ready to fight. I notice that my nails have grown longer and are now covered in blood and fur. I can feel that my fangs are extended in my mouth. I have never had this happen before.

I look down at Cadence who is unconscious. He has transformed into a white cat-like creature with light blue eyes.

I watch as his body slowly changes back to his man form. I pay no mind to the two others which are standing by me.

"You must come with us. There will be more of them soon. They'll smell the blood and more will come. We must go and seek shelter." One of the male says to me. I nod.

"Yes. Please help me get him out of here and I will go with you." I agree feeling I have no other choice but to get off of the darken tundra and away from the endless danger it offers.

Ω

I cautiously follow the two cloaked stranger as they lead me through an openly in a grass covered hill I hadn't noticed before. A large boulder concealed a hidden underground carven. Once inside a torch is lit by one of the males. As the light from the torch grows the small cave is filled with light revealing our rescuers faces to me for the first time. I have Cade over my shoulder and his weight is getting to me so lay him down on the cave floor. One of them assemblies together a small fire and heat from it begins to cause Cade to stir.

"Cade, are you hurt?" I ask into his ear while bent over him. He shifts back and forth but his eyes remain closed. "Just rest now. Don't try to move, Cade." I assure. The two males remove their cloaks finally revealing their faces. One of them sits beside Cade. He is a ferlin I notice. I have never seen one in person. He is covered in green scales with diamond shaped pupils in the middle of a green eye. He pulls something out from underneath his clothing before applying what appears to be a liquid.

"*Niche matten tu*?" He asks me in his native tongue.

"I don't understand your language I'm afraid." I shake my head. "But if that is something that will heal him please do so immediately!" I plea. I know that probably he doesn't understand me but I must try.

"He doesn't speak Kyscon but I can understand all the languages of the Kysco Nation." The second male says to me. He joins us on the cave floor before pulling out a flame and setting it on the burn. The flame heat increases filling the cave with its whit glow and the warmth from it starts to warm Cade flesh. I place my hands on his bare back noticing he is warming to the right temperature. His clothes are torn and what little cloth that remains is covered in blood from those night creatures.

"He needs to be covered in wraps or he'll freeze to death."

"I'm so cold!" His blue lips moan.

"We have turned the flame on you it will warm you up soon." I slump my head down towards his ear. "The flame heat will make you better." I lie. I have not ever had to use a flame before my skin doesn't require artificial heat. Cade's skin seems to be fragile like the flesh of the royal council. The ferlin turns the flame up and the heat immediately increases.

"*Tarcon ush...*" He speaks in his native tongue. I nod even know I don't understand him. He seems to be trying to help Cade and I'm grateful. Dahlia only spoke of the ferlin a few times. She told me how ferlin are great hunters even though they are plant eaters.

"*Tarcon ush tu wei.*" He replies before pulling something from his robe before placing it on the ground next to Cade. I think I can decipher what he's saying a little in that the wants to help. The other male looks at me.

"*Tarcon* will help your heal. He has been bitten by the sphinx. Their venom is deadly if we don't treat those bites he will parish before the rise of the yellow hue." He reaches down placing his fingertips into the small pouch before removing a clear ointment. He looks at me for approval first, I nod giving it. He massages it onto Cade leaving no wound untreated.

Ω

After several hours Cade starts to open his eyes.

"Where are we? What is this place, Aria?" He pulls his body up off the ground and flexes his glare on me. His wounds appear to be gone and he seems physically fit again.

"We are safe for now, Cade. These males helped us with those creatures."

"Sphinx." The white skinned male says.

"These males helped kill those sphinx but you were bitten by one and the venom made you pass out." I point at his arm. He looks over his body.

"I have no wounds...and I think that I was probably just having one hell of a hallucination that I was a tiger." He chuckles as my eyes widen knowing the name of the animal that Cade changed in to.

"Yes, Cade that happened it was no hallucination, you changed into a tiger and you killed a bunch of those sphinx all by yourself."

"You are a two-skin." The white skinned male adds. I have heard that name before but I don't know when, possible a story that Dahlia told me.

Suddenly, the loose dirt underneath the boulder blocking the cave entry starts moving. The two males jump to their feet.

"*Man boose oui*!" *Neei wush*!" The ferlin shouts.

"We must go further into the cave! Your mates been marked with the sphinx scent and they have tracked him here. They can dig their way in here soon. We must hide deeper in the cave."

"*Mai mai*!"

"Sean, says there's water deeper inside this cave." The white skinned male says as they both head into the dark entry heading deeper into the cave, Cade stands pursuing the two others.

I look at the cave entry as more loose dirt spills into the cave and I can hear the snarling and growling of several sphinx just outside. Their eager paws digging together wanting nothing more than to make us their meal I can sense. I do not think I could fight all them off this time.

"Are you coming, Aria?" Cade shouts from inside the tunnel.

"Yes...Yes I'm coming."

Chapter 10

The bursting curiosity of knowing that I transformed that I in fact changed into a tiger has me eagerly following these two strangers. Aria is walking alongside me through this narrowing tunnel.

I notice the further we go the more I have to duck down finally I have to push Aria ahead of me because I have no more space on the sides of us to go two by two. I can hear echoes of the sphinx hallowing just beyond us and it seems they are nearing us.

"They must have dug their way into the cave." I say aloud.

"Hurry there's an opening up ahead here!" I hear one of them yell from ahead.

"I can hear the water, Cade we must be close." Aria says as I squat down while increasing my speed another few hundred feet with little to no light to see around me. I can only feel the sides of the tunnel as it opens up and I can see Aria standing in a huge cave corridor. Sean pulls out something that lights up and I can see the entire corridor perfectly.

There's a pool of water at the other end of the corridor.

"We must get into the water and stay in the water it's the only thing that will keep them from killing us. They won't go into the water." The normal skinned man says as he and his lizard-like skinned friend get into the water submerging them neck high. I love swimming so I have no issues going for a swim in this underground cavern. The light from their lamp glows under the water showing the vast beautiful blue color.

Both Aria and I follow them into the water joining them on the other side of the cavern just as ten or more sphinx burst into the cavern opening racing over to the waters' edge growling and snarling and just like they said they halted only by the water.

"We will need to figure out another way out of this cavern." I say before I dive under the water swimming over to the deeper part looking for some sort of exit. After a few seconds with no luck I come up for air. Aria is there looking at me.

"I will find a way out, Cade." She says before disappearing under the water. I lose sight of her for several minutes.

"Who can hold their breath that long?" I yell aloud.

"Breeders can." The man says like he knows everything about Aria's race and he probably does.

Before I can get out another question Aria pops her head up out of the water.

"Over here, there's a way out over here. There's just enough space at the top of this small tunnel for you all to breath but in another few hundred meters the tunnel opens up again into another cavern. We should be able to get out that way." Aria says before we all follow her, me going last.

Ω

All of us are clinging to the tunnel roof accessing those few inches of breathing space while we fiercely make our way towards the unknown. I try not to swallow too much water as I paddle my arms forward quickly following Aria as closely as possible. The water goes up my nose causing me to choke a bit as I unintentionally take in water.

"Shit!" I gag and cough. I hear the others behind coughing as well but their light continues to follow me shining the way and lighting up the blue vast bottom below us. I effortlessly swim completely accustom to the warm temperature of the water. It's like an underground grotto as the tunnel opens up leading us into a larger carven. Aria swims over to the edge of the water pulling her body up and out of the water with ease.

"Come on over. There appears to be away out over here." Aria says. I follow her out of the water noticing the two others right behind me doing the same. I'm dripping wet and cold.

"Wait, is it safe outside? Those sphinx are still out there I bet just waiting to attack us." I stop in my tracks with both the others pausing alongside me.

Aria turns to us and nods without protest we all sit down to make camp for what I hope is a short night.

"Well, it looks like we have made out of that alive. I think that was the closest we have been to dying in a long time, Sean." Felix says to Sean.

"Tragons killas ut ash, Felix." Sean says back to Felix.

"I for one am very grateful to the both of you for helping me out here with those sphinx creatures. My name is Cadence Troy; it is a pleasure to meet you two. As you can probably tell I'm not from around here." I say.

"Nice to meet you Cadence Troy, I'm Felix and this here (he points to Sean) is Sean. I am from the Shylo farmlands. And Sean here is from the underneath which is the underground caverns underneath the Shylo Tribe ruins. He is ferlin an under-dweller." Felix says.

"I am Aria, from the fortress of the Kysco Nation. I'm a breeder." Aria says.

"I know that you are a breeder. Well, I'm thrilled to meet your acquaintance." Felix says.

"Tragons killas." Killas ist zu." Sean says in some language I can't even try to understand.

"No Sean she will not eat us." Felix says back to Sean.

"What do you mean by eat you? Is that what you think I will do is eat you? No, I only drink from the Yukon Sea, and even if I get really hungry I would never hurt anyone, I can only drink from a willing participant so tell Sean that he is completely safe with me."

"Don't let him bother you, Aria he doesn't mean anything by it. Sean and I have had a dangerous life here out on the tundra; he always believed that breeders are dangerous ever since he was a boy. Back before we meet." Felix says.

"Have you two always known one another?" I ask.

"Why would he believe? Does he know that breeders are the source of all life? We are chosen at birth out of millions to deliver a new race to the Kysco Nation." Aria says.

"Killas Nation zu." Sean says.

"Sean, I'm not going to tell her that." Felix says.

"Zu Zu Tragons killas und." Sean says.

"Fine but she's not going to understand what I'm saying she's too young and she doesn't know the truth."

"Zu und..." Sean starts to say.

"Enough of this back and forth and just tell me what Sean told you to tell me. What truth will I not understand? Why is he afraid of my kind?" Aria cuts in.

"Aria, your kind feeds on his race. At least your kind used to until the ferlin were no more. Sean said that not all breeders act like or look like you do, Aria." Felix says. Aria's eyes widen and fill with water and it looks like she might cry. "Some breeders are evil and furious. They killed almost the entire ferlin race. Now only a few remain, and only by leaving behind their homes and fleeing the underneath. On the day me and Sean met I was only a baby practically a newborn when Sean's father and him found me." Felix says.

"Gut tag, meinen Felix." Sean says.

"I don't understand what you all are talking about for sure but I can say that I don't feel the least bit afraid to be around Aria nor do I believe that she could possibly be any harm to anyone. Maybe your friend Sean got it work and maybe since he was so young, he just made a mistake and he just thought that they were breeders that killed his race off." I say as I start feel like I need to stand up for her somehow.

"Yes this must be the answer, Felix listen to Cade he has been here with me and he would not feel safe with me if I was a killer as you say I am." Aria says not looking at me.

"Yes I feel perfectly safe with her and so should you two." I add.

Ω

Beads of sweat rolled down my forehead urging me to rub my head with the light blue hanker-cuff that my aunt Maggie gave me. I can hear my grandfather humming his favorite tune while he steers The Last Star his schooner. My lips are wet with dew from the spray of the ocean's waves while it blasts against the boat's front end. I hold on tighter as we sail further out to sea. I'm perched up front like I'm the nose of the boat, swimming, diving and leading way.

A foreign sound makes me realize that I'm dreaming and in a flash I'm in my adult self watching the day. I notice my grandfather pull something from his pocket and the sunlight catches it causing the necklace to beam sunlight onto my little kid eyes. I stand still as my younger self runs right through my adult self as if I'm not real. My kid self dashes over to my grandfather who quickly fastens the necklace chain around my very small neck. I place my own hand to my neck felling for that chain and then I remember how it heated up just before it began to glow just before I was sent here. I stir myself awake with the thought and open my eyes. Aria is gone from my side.

I sit up panicked scanning the cavern for her before seeing her off standing near the cave exit standing watch over us I assume. I spot the other two men sleeping one closer to me and the other is closer to the exit sleeping sitting up.

Chapter 11

I see Cade is awake and I'm immediately relieved but I don't understand why. He joins me by the cave exit. From this point I see out of the there and I can tell that there is only a short distance between us and the opening to the cave. I had thought about going out of the cave for hours while the others slept but didn't have the chance to.

"Did you go out there yet to see what is outside?" Cade asks me.

"No, I didn't want risk leaving you unguarded while the others slept." I say.

"I'm not a baby you know, I can take care of myself. I've been taking care of myself for over two decades now." his words fly at my face and it's obvious I've upset him a bit.

"I don't mean to upset you, Cade I apologize." I say and his face softens.

"Ha ha. No, please don't apologize it is me who should apologize I'm being rude." He replies. "Probably that dream messing with my head and my emotions." He says quieter. "I'm sorry, Aria for snapping at you just now." He adds.

"You should be ferocious with me given our current circumstances that I put us into." I ask.

"What? No, this circumstance isn't your fault, Aria." He says.

"Yes, it is my fault because I put us here by following the orders I thought I was given but I must have been wrong Cade, and I'm a liar too." I add but turn away from him as I walk out of the cave exiting from the first time.

I can hear him right behind me. I feel his warm breath on my neck. I slow down allowing him to catch up to me. The passage is narrow but big enough for me and Cade to walk alongside each other. The walls end and the passage way is now covered in vines and branches which I break away with my hands clearing them out of the way. Suddenly, the passageway is filled with the light of the yellow hue.

"Look Cade, it is now safe to travel again when the yellow hue is in the sky and the sphinx should all be gone for now." I assure him.

"Good, I'm glad it's morning again." He gives his own name to the yellow hue by calling it morning.

"I like this name, morning. I will use it as well." I say and he looks at me strangely.

"Why did you call yourself a liar, Aria?" He asks.

"I have been telling you that I know what I'm doing but I don't know anything about this place because I have never been here and until today I only know that this place was a childhood story told to me by my guide Dahlia." I spill all my truths to him. I break through the exit and walk outside the purple and yellow hues are now in the sky. "I think that we can make it to the Shylo tribe village before the next blue hue."

"If you say so than I believe you." Cade says.

"We will not make it to the Shylo tribe city before the harvest hue, no one can travel that fast." Felix says as he joins us awaken obviously by the light of yellow hue.

"What is the harvest hue?" Cade asks.

This is a term I'm familiar with; it is the day I was to be chosen and mated by the royal council member who I now believe is dead. Too many thoughts start circling in my head at once I can't make sense of any of them.

"Harvest hue is what the Kysco Nation calls it and yes, either name you use it means the same thing for us, three full days of the blue hue which makes it a perfect time for feeding and for the night creatures to feed off of all of us. And then they will come and they will....." Felix says and his words explain some but leave us hanging like his afraid to finish. He looks away from me and at the ground. "The purged come during the harvest. That's the purpose for the harvest hue." He adds.

"Great so we're the ones being harvested than?" Cade says as he gathers more data as I should have known but somehow I've been living under a cloak of much prettier pictures.

"What is the purged?" I ask.

"The purged are a blood thirsty Army of the Kysco Nation." They are the ones the Sean was talking about earlier.

"Wait a minute you mean to tell me that there's an army of creatures that feeds on people like us?" Cade presses.

"No they won't eat her just us. That's if we are still out in the open where they can easily smell us and find us. Plus, the sphinx will be out hunting us again too. I must get to my farm where we will be safe." Flex explains and I nod my head without thinking because I have no other better plan and precious moments are passing.

"I will follow you to your farm if Cade can get something to eat and he is safe there." I say.

"Hmm, maybe we should continue on our own way. Those things won't hurt you and well I can change back into a tiger surely keeping up with you. Look I'm completely healed now." He points to his healed body.

"How long will it take us to get to the Shylo Tribe city from here?" Cade asks Felix.

"We are at last two fall hues from the village and the first harvest will start tonight at the blue hue rise. That means no matter how fast you two can run you will be out in the open during the harvest and I don't advice it. You should come back with us." Felix says.

"Cade, I must agree with Felix we are not safe out in the open at night no matter what." I add.

"Fine, I will come along than I hope you have some meat to eat because I could certainly eat right now." Cade groans and I hear his belly growl.

"You are hungry of course I had forgotten that." I say to myself. *Cade hasn't eaten anything other than the small hand full of shylo berries I brought him some time ago.*

"Yes, Cade I do have meat and milk for you to eat at my farm."

Ω

"Felix this shank tastes just like chicken which I used to have all the time from my world." Cade shreds through another serving of shank meat that all of them are eating except me.

"Don't think I forgot about you, Aria." Felix says before filling my mug with Yukon Sea water. I drink down all of it at once finding myself fully nourished and reenergized as it appears Cade is as well.

"I can't believe that's what you live off of, Aria." Cade's lip recoils.

I think the same about the shank meat and shank birds. I don't say anything but rather I smile at him and Felix who pours me another full mug.

"Thank you, Felix for feeding us and for saving us from those sphinx." I add before burying my face behind the mug.

"Yes thank you Felix for everything. And please thank Sean for helping to heal me from the sphinx venom."

I had forgotten about that ointment that Sean had used on Cade. I don't think I've ever seen anyone hurt before so that was the first I had see someone given body aid. I believe that if it were not for Sean, Cade would have died as a cause of the sphinx venom. At this point I am not sure if Cade is safe with me anymore; maybe I should leave him here with these two. I consider my options silently.

"Felix could you please sketch me a map to the shylo city; I'd like see what kind distance I might be facing under the blue hue." I ask.

"You say that as if you are planning on traveling to the city without me, Aria?" Cade nudges my arm with his.

"No I won't leave you behind." I lie to him all the while *I'm thinking I don't like our changes but I don't want to leave him for any reason as silly as it sounds in my head. I feel obligated to him and I don't want to let him down. I don't want to see him hurt again and I know these two can't fight as well as I can. They can't keep Cade safe like I can.* I battle back and forth with my thoughts.

"Yes but I don't need to sketch you a map though, Aria I already have a map of the whole realm, including all three tribal ranges."

I nod my head as if I understand what he is talking about.

"I'd love to get a look at that map myself. I'm getting tired of tripping through strange tundra's not sure which way is which." Cade says to me before making a strange sound and the others join him.

I can't blame him not wanting to blindly follow me, plus I nearly got him killed and I forgot to feed him because I forgot he eats food. I watch him as he digs into some bread that is over on the counter. Felix spreads the map open on the table in front of me. I stand leaning over it taking it all in entirely. I notice the words and symbols but I can't understand their meaning.

"Where are the three tribes on this map Felix?" I press my hands down on the bottom of the map careful not to cover anything up. He points to three different spots while saying, "Kysco, Shylo, Darjin tribes," he finishes with a smile like Cade always does.

"I see and over here is where we are then?" I point to the range on the map where I think we are now.

"Yes, that is correct Aria. Here I'll leave this out for you to study. You should be as familiar with your nation. The Kysco Nation rules over the entire realm." Felix adds before sitting back down.

"Wow, Aria by the way you're looking at this map I'd say you're just as unfamiliar with this place as I am." Cade's voice cracks from behind me.

"I've just never seen it on a map before." I snap. I'm sure that he can see through my fake assurances at this point but I will continue to pretend a little bit longer. He seems content with my answer as he settles back in his chair with an empty plate in front of him.

"Do you want more meat, Cade? I can make more if you are still hungry." Felix asks.

"No thank you Felix I'm afraid my stomach might burst open if I have another bite." They both make the same sounds as before. I don't look up while they seem to be moving around the room. I need to memorize this map so I'll never be lost again nor feel like a stranger in my own land. I see that I have traveled very far away from the Kysco fortresses were I was raised. I can also see that I am very close to the Shylo city. I want to leave right now according to this map I could be in Shylo Tribe city reuniting with Dahlia by tomorrow at the very latest considering my speed and all. I of course would need to leave Cade here. He'd be better off with these males than he is with me. Plus, he will only slow me down and I will probably get him killed. I look up briefly seeing them gathered over by the window. I look back at the map. I should probably wait until the blue hue starts and they are all asleep that is when I can slip away.

"Hey, Aria you need to see this. Hurry, come over here and take a look at this!" Cade demands and I don't budge. "Aria?" Cade repeats.

"What I'm busy over here?" I say.

"You'll want to see this trust me, Aria!"

Chapter 12

I can't believe my eyes while standing at the window with Felix and Sean watching what can only be described as an eclipse of the three moons or hues as Aria calls them. The purple moon moves slowly in front of the huge blue ringed moon which completely covers up the yellow and the smallest moon. I'm nearly frozen in place not wanting to miss a thing.

"Aria, hurry you have to see this." I beg her again with my eyes fixed on the marvelous sight in the sky. "Oh wait a minute." I put my eyes downward. "Is it ok to just look directly at the hues?" I ask Felix.

"Yes, you can look at them as they become one darken blue hue, Cade."

I hear Aria answer as she joins us at the window.

"You have eyes just like those of the Kysco Nation, like the royal council and they have a huge ceremony once a spin to celebrate the harvest hue."

"It is a very deadly time for our villages and that's the exact time the royal council celebrates. We become food if we are not careful." Felix jumps in. "You probably need to eat something to, Aria." He adds before leaving to fetch something I don't look to see what. "It is almost time for it to began." Felix says to Sean from behind us. I hear Sean say something quietly in his language which I don't understand still and therefore I have started tuning it out. I realize that I am now starting to feel my withdrawal symptoms starting with my old friend irritability. I will pretend as if I'm not pissed off for any reason and right now my inability to understand Sean is all I can take. I push my fingers down on the window seal. I see the appearance of the white knuckles on my tan hands. My secret desire is back screaming in my ear, and it's screaming for booze. For as long as I can remember I've started and ended everyday with my secret desire by my side. Now I'm stuck here and up until this very moment I had no withdrawal symptoms. "What happened?" I whisper to myself. Aria shoots me a quick side look but says nothing. She already thinks of me as a weakling and now these withdrawals will really show her my biggest weakness of all. I got to do something quick before this gets worse. Maybe if I can get a hold of more shylo berries I can suppress my withdrawals symptoms.

"We could use your help preparing for the three days of the hue." Felix calls from his front door. My mind scrambles.

"Absolutely, Felix do you think I could trouble you for some Shylo berries first?"

"I'll give you something much more potent than berries Cade." He shouts while exiting leaving me no choice but to follow him all along wondering what the hell could be stronger than those berries. Whatever his offer is what I need to get me by. I don't notice that Aria is on my trail until I catch up to Felix outside on the edge of his fields.

"Why is your heart racing, are you scared, Cade?" She asks me why looking at me as though I'm a kid.

"How do you know my heart is racing Aria?" Can you actually hear it beating in my chest or something?" I laugh at the thought.

"Yes, actually I can hear your heart beating in your chest and I can hear your lungs expanding and filling with air too. I can hear most of everything, Cade.

"Here..." Felix hands me a mug of a dark liquid. "As I promised here's something better then Shylo berries."

I smell it and drink it. "Shylo berry rum." He finishes.

I hear only the word rum and immediately down the entire contents. Did he say rum? As the dark liquid follows into my blood stream I start swimming in warm thoughts.

"I love Shylo berry rum, damn! Thank you, Felix this is hitting the spot very nicely indeed." As he promised the rum starts working on me immediately. I feel stronger and my head is clearer. I don't know if it is the rum or the anticipation of the harvest hue and what will happen next.

"What is wrong with you?" Aria snaps quietly in my ear. The suddenness of makes me jump. "Calm down...why are jumping around Cade?" She adds while pulling back her hand I fear to slap me again.

"Don't hit me again, Aria I'm just fine. I'm actually better than fine, I'm great!" She pulls me closer

"You are intoxicated."

Before I can get even one word out a bright glow grabs my eye and all my attention. I turn just as a wall of fire ignites, rolling in a perfect line for a mile or so until Felix's entire property line is fully a blaze.

I must be drunk I realize as I can't look away from the beauty of the wall of fire which they have set I assume as our first line of defense against the night creatures. The fire burn is so bright that I had not noticed the full eclipse of the three moons bringing the darkness.

"We should get back inside now the harvest has begun, soon they will come." Felix adds his final warning before setting back towards his home. Confused and dazed I follow behind with

Aria at my side. She hasn't spoken since the full eclipse I think she's actually speechless.

"Have you seen this before, the harvest hue I mean?" I ask but she remains quiet. "Are you alright, Aria? Are you scared now?"

"Be quiet Cade, I'm listening to the sounds around us." She says before quicken her pace.

"What sounds?" I say quieter.

"I can hear..." She stops in her tracks.

"You can hear...what exactly?" I ask. Her big eyes find mine.

"I can hear them all and they are coming straight for us."

I don't need to know the names of the monsters nor do I want to but press anyways.

"Are they the same things from yesterday...those sphinx things again?"

"Yes and many others. I need more strength, Cade. I need to eat or I will not be able to fight them all."

"Okay we will get you some more ox blood then."

"No I need the waters of the Yukon."

"Well we're nowhere near the Yukon anymore, Aria."

"I need to drink from you again if there's no Yukon. I need fresh blood the fresher the better."

"What? Seriously you want to drink my blood?"

"Please it will not hurt you at all. It will make me stronger and it will help you too you'll see." She leans towards my neck, I allow her not knowing why but I feel overwhelmed by the promise of the return of that previous pleasure. Her fangs sink down into my neck and I feel them enter my skin. It stings at first but it quickly fades into a shuttle cooling sensation which ends with a nice tingling thumb. Pulling back she comes eye to eye with me.

"Now we can face the herd of beasts." Aria says.

To Be Continued

The Survivor

Bloods Divide Universe II

Chapter 1

My strength is fully restored to the highest level now that I have had fresh blood from Cade. I can now hear and see that we are outnumbered and that the night creatures approaching us are much larger than the sphinx.

"What can you hear, Aria? Can you see them yet? How many of them are there?" Cade asks me and I look at him unsure how to express the seriousness of the situation.

"Cade, I can hear and see them all and we are outnumbered and unevenly matched. You're going to need to change into your other skin, Cade now if you can. Then maybe we might stand a chance for a little while." I say as Cade immediately transforms right before my eyes into a white cat which he calls a tiger. "Oh, wow Cade you look ready for battle now." I say to his tiger form and he growls up at me almost trying to speak.

"I can't believe that we are lucky even to have a two-skin with us on the harvest hue. Now at least we will have a fighting chance. Well, at until my sister Breeyan comes to get us that is." Felix says.

"Your sister is coming here now to get you?" I ask uncertain how a Shyloian could possibly be strong enough to actual rescue all of us from the night creatures.

"Yes, my sister Breeyan has a tundra runner and she can take us all to Shylo City in no time. See so there's no need to go out on your own as I said before we are safest here until she arrives." Felix says.

"Did you just say she has a object that can run fast? What is a tundra runner? I have never heard of such a thing. Dahlia never told me about those." I ask Felix who doesn't seem shocked by my questions.

"A tundra runner can fly us all to safety and now that the harvest hue is amongst us she knows to come and get us. My sister would never leave us to die here." Felix says.

Just then a dark cloud appears above our heads

"Look out its shank above." Felix shouts. Their sounds are loud. "If they are here soon so will more meat eaters." Felix warns.

Cade becomes violent and starts to pace back and forth while leaping up to try and catch one of the shank from the air but misses it. He must be to smell them and he might recognize their smell from before when he was eating them for supper in his man form.

"I gather you probably want to eat more of those shank uh, Cade?" I say to the tiger form of him to which he growls loudly just before leaping to try to catch one from the air...

More of, *The Survivor*

From author
Stacy McCarty

I SINCERELY HOPE THAT you have enjoyed reading The Traveler, from the Bloods Divides Universe. It was an absolute pleasure writing this book. This is the first paranormal sci-fi title I have written, and I plan on continuing this journey for many years to come.

Please let me know what I can do to further improve my writing or simply say "way to go girl", by leaving me a review. Your feedback and comments will help me with my success. Review The Traveler here.

Character List and abilities

CADENCE/CADE TROY

Race: Half human earthling and half two-skin.

Age: 44 spins 22 earth years

Description: Black hair, brown eyes, tan complexion, approximately 168 pounds, six foot one inch tall, slightly muscular body type.

Abilities: He is a two-skin shifter who shifts into white tiger. He has photographic memory, and he advanced with electronics he hides how smart he is pretending to be dumb. He is an admitted alcoholic.

ARIA

Race: Tragons

Age: 40 spins 20 earth years

Description: Dark Blonde hair, blue-purple eyes, tan complexion, approximately 118 pounds, five foot three inches tall, curvy hips with a muscular body type.

Abilities: She has the strength of ten men, can run at the speed of light making her invisible which is about thirty-eight thousand miles per hour but she can only maintain that speed for a minimal time because of the planets pressure. She can see in the dark and hold her breath for two hours. She can appear dead for days if necessary. She can speak and understand all the languages of Tragon after she hears them for a while, a true linguist. She can transfer her powers temporary to the person who she shares her blood with. She can hear sounds for up to twenty miles away. To the world she is to be left untouched and unharmed but to the Kysco Nation royal council that is lucky even to mate with her, they will have full reign over her forever. She is also immortal.

Dahlia

Race: Tragons

Age: 84 spins 42 earth years

Description: Black hair, brown eyes, light complexion, approximately 148 pounds, five foot ten inches tall, slightly muscular body type.

Abilities: same as Aria but more advanced because of her age.

Felix Mapping

Race: Shyloian

Age: 30 spins 15 earth years

Description: Silver hair, gray eyes, pale white complexion, approximately 185 pounds, six foot three inches tall, slightly muscular body type with some extra weight from age.

Abilities: Good with the cross bow and hunting night creature. An excellent farmer and botanist making him in control of the majority of sproutshroom and Shylo berries in the Shylo region, he is similar looking to humans from earth.

Sean

Race: Ferlin

Age: 84 spins 42 earth years

Description: No hair, green eyes, lizard type skin covering his body, approximately 205 pounds, six foot tall, very muscular body type and has no tail.

Abilities: A native to the underneath which is under dwellings of the Oldlands. It believed that ferlins are as old as the Tragons. He is a great hunter and life-long friends with Felix.

Judy

Race: Human from earth

Age: 44 spins 22 earth years

Abilities: She a good friend and normal human being. Best friends to Cadence since high school, she was there for him during the most painful times of his life.

Royal council

Race: Humans from earth

Age: 84 spins 42 earth years

Description: No hair, green eyes, lizard type skin covering his body, approximately 205 pounds, six foot tall, very muscular body type and has no tail.

Abilities: Humans from earth, they have intelligential weapons and an android called a dagger to protect them.

Breeyan Mapping

Race: Shyloian

Age: 44 spins 22 earth years

Description: Red hair, green eyes, pale complexion, approximately 125 pounds, five foot six inches tall, extra weight around belly and untrained.

Abilities:

Aunt Maggie

Race: Human

Age: 164 spins 82 earth years

Description: White hair, blue eyes, tan complexion, approximately 105 pounds, five foot two inches tall, slender and very frail.

Abilities: Good community leader, sister, cousin, and wife. No children but she helped raise Cadence once his father and mother went missing when he was a toddler.

Bloods Divide

Glossary of Terms

- Breeder: Tragons kidnapped at birth an advance race cross bread with the sole purpose of mating a superior race.
- Dagger: Trained android protector to the breeders and their mated council member.
- Darjin: Magical native mammal similar to earthlings.
- Dark Creatures: A name for the many different deadly creatures that hunt at night on the tundra of the Kysco Nation.
- Drone: Devices used by the royal council that has a camera used for tracking and spying on others. Operated by dagger.
- Fae: Any creature or mammal with the ability to perform magic.
- Flame: A device that provides heat.
- Fly: flying, running fast for Breeders, daggers and Guides.
- Guide: Teacher of Tragon children offering training on how to become a breeder.
- Hues: The three small moons one with large ring orbiting Tragon and the light and heat source.

- Kysco Nation: The large most populated region on Tragon.
- Kyscon: The language spoken by the royal council and it is the law that everyone must speak it or is arrested or killed.
- Oldlands: Shylo tribe ruins abandon by the elders of the old tribes.
- Purged: The mutated offspring of cross-bread Tragons with anything other than royal council.
- Royal Council: Self appointed superior race in control of the Kysco Nation and all surrounding regions.
- Shank: A bird found on Tragon that tastes like chicken.
- Shylo berry: An edible white blossom with a thick fruity stem, similar flavor to mangos.
- Shylo: A race of mammals, similar to the humans of Earth. Usually farmers or engineers.
- Shyloian: The spoken dialectic of the Shylo race.
- Sphinx: A venoms night creature that looks like a scaled hairless dog.
- Spin: The timeframe equal to one year on earth.
- Sproutshroom: A small white or grey fungus sprout which is farmed and sold for currency by Shylo farmers. Normally grows in the open warm climates.
- Tarcon: a clear colored mud from the caves underneath the Shylo ruins, used for healing.
- Torch: A small or large device that provides light.
- Tragon: The planet Aria is from.
- Tragons: advanced species with superhuman abilities that once ruled the entire region and the only true native to the Ksyon Nation.
- Tundra runner: A vehicle that hovers six or more feet off the ground which is used for transportation by the Shlyoians in secret. It can reach speeds of one hundred and eighty miles per hour.
- Tundra: Flat land that is mostly rocky or has some dirt covered small hills without trees, only some small plant life.

· Two-skins: A human who can shift into an animal. Some can shift into multiple animals.

· Vampire: Cade version of breeders, old folklore not real.

· Zerkers: Crazed half-wolf half beast-man over seven feet tall and weighing three or more hundred pounds, one of the night creatures on the Kysco Nation tundra.

Dedications

I dedicated this book to the world for being so damn boring so that I wanted to make up my own world equipped with monsters and vampire-aliens.

Stalk this author

YOU ARE MORE THAN WELCOME to follow me please, I want you to.

Website

Facebook Page

Facebook Profile

Twitter

Instagram

Email

All titles from this author

THE TRAVELER

Bloods Divide Universe I

The Survivor

The Traveler Series

Bloods Divide Universe II

Release date April

The Two Skins

The Traveler Series

Bloods Divide Universe III

Release date April

The Darjin

The Traveler Series

Bloods Divide Universe IV

Release date May

AND MORE COMING SOON...

Complete Backlist

Don't miss out!

Visit the website below and you can sign up to receive emails whenever Stacy McCarty publishes a new book. There's no charge and no obligation.

https://books2read.com/r/B-A-VCUKC-TMQKF

BOOKS 2 READ

Connecting independent readers to independent writers.

Also by Stacy McCarty

Bloods Divide Universe
The Traveler

Rapture of Men
Thorn
Pestilence

About the Author

Rapture of Men, authored by ***Stacy McCarty***, serves as the gripping sequel in this chilling series that delves into the harrowing themes of apocalyptic horror intertwined with supernatural elements and a spine-tingling paranormal romance. The narrative plunges readers into a world teetering on the brink of destruction, where the eerie atmosphere and unsettling occurrences heighten the tension, drawing them deeper into a tale that explores the darker facets of love and survival amidst chaos.

www.ingramcontent.com/pod-product-compliance
Lightning Source LLC
LaVergne TN
LVHW052053160826
845678LV00015B/3198

* 9 7 9 8 2 2 7 1 6 8 9 8 6 *